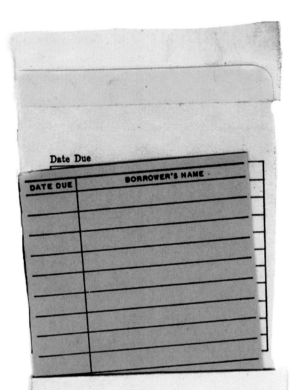

Date Due

DATE DUE	BORROWER'S NAME	

Rosie the Reader

To Hailey,
Never stop reading!
♡

Dedications

For Norah and Henry – love you to the
moon and back.
J. Baker-Smith

For Prince John-John and Princess Mia --
wisdom, mercy, and peace, and may the
stars dance at your feet.
J. Moorer

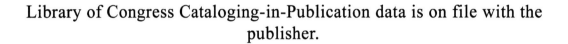

Library of Congress Cataloging-in-Publication data is on file with the
publisher.

Text copyright © 2018 by Joanne Baker-Smith
Pictures copyright © 2018 by John Moorer
Published in 2018 by Baker-Smith Publishers and Moorerland Studios
in connection with Createspace

ISBN 1-9862-3980-2   EAN 978-1-9862-3980-6

Printed in the United States

Design by John Moorer and Annie Douvas

Little Learner Series · Book One

Rosie the Reader

Written By Joanne Baker-Smith
Illustrated By John Moorer

It was another exciting day in room 129.
Rosie sat happily at her desk.

"Tomorrow, I will start testing everyone's reading level," Ms. Smith said with a smile.

Rosie loved reading, but was a little nervous about a test.

When her mom got home from work, she told her all about the reading test.

"You're ready for this!" her mother said with a smile. "Just think about how much you practice each day."

**"You read with Daddy each morning
before he goes to work."**

"You and Ollie read to each other on the bus each morning."

"When you get to school, you tell Grace about the books you read with Ollie."

**"At lunch, you practice your sight words
with Luke and Lia."**

"You and Grandpa go on word hunts all around the neighborhood while walking home from school."

"After you finish your homework, you play word games with Grandma."

"You read to me while I am cooking dinner each night."

"You are ready!" Mom said confidently. Rosie hugged her mom tightly. "Thanks Mom!" Rosie whispered.

Rosie went to get her book baggie.
She rushed back to her mom and asked,
"Want to hear me read?"
"Yes!" Mom said with a smile.

The next day during reading time, Rosie smiled when her teacher called her name to be tested. "I'm ready for this!" Rosie said to herself as she walked over to her teacher.

**When Rosie was done reading for her
teacher, she told her all about the story.**

Her teacher smiled, "Well done Rosie!
You moved up two reading levels!"

Rosie went back to her desk with a smile. She couldn't wait to get home and tell her family!

Reader's Page

Now that you have finished Rosie the Reader, get out there and read! Here are some great ways to grow as a reader.

Reading Ideas

*Have a parent, grandparent, sibling, or friend read a higher level story out loud to model great reading.

*Take turns reading aloud with a partner (try using silly voices). Pick a page, sentence, or a character and read those parts.

*Have a parent, grandparent, sibling or friend read a page from your book aloud first then you reread it.

Retell Ideas

*Retell your story by sharing the important events in the beginning, middle, and end with someone.

*Try to see if you can tell your story across your hand (five finger retell). Each finger represents an important part of the story.

*Act out your favorite part with family or friends.

*Explain to a parent, guardian, sibling, or friend what the problem was in the story and how the character /characters solved it.

Sight Word Games

*Write your sight words on index cards (write each word twice) and play memory. Write the words, turn them over, and then try to make a match.

*Walk around the neighborhood/store with an adult and see how many sight words you can find. Keep track and see who can find the most.

*Try writing your words in sand or in paint to help feel the letters.

*Draw a picture to go with your work and create your own sight word book.

*Write your words in the colors of the rainbow. Start with writing the word in red, then trace over with orange, yellow, green, blue, indigo, and finally violet.

*Don't forget there are a ton of great ideas and information on the internet!

About the Author

Joanne Baker-Smith is an elementary school teacher, health & wellness coach, and author. She has taught in the NYC public school system for over 12 years. It was within this time as an early childhood teacher where she began to notice areas and situations that made her young students feel concerned about their abilities. She utilized strategies to empower them and give them confidence in their learning. It is these strategies that inspired Joanne's creation of the Little Learner Series to help children beyond her classroom feel as good about learning as her own students did. She lives in Forest Hills, New York with her husband and two children.

About the Illustrator

John Moorer; born in New York City, and raised on a steady diet of comic books, music, and philosophy. His favorite forms of art include traditional watercolors, acrylics, and both physicial and digital sketching. With a love of the human figure and a passion for storytelling, you can usually find John writing or drawing something around his home in Long Island, New York.
Website, JohnMoorer.com
Follow on Instagram, @JohnMoorerArt

Made in the USA
Lexington, KY
24 May 2018